Big Jake

Dave and Pat Sargent are longtime residents of Prairie Grove, Arkansas. Dave, a fourth-generation dairy farmer, began writing in early December of 1990, and Pat, a former teacher, began writing in the fourth grade. They enjoy the outdoors and have a real love for animals.

Big Jake

Animal Pride Series
Book 12

By

Dave and Pat Sargent

Beyond The End
By
Sue Rogers

Illustrated by
Jeane Lirley Huff

Ozark Publishing, Inc.
P.O. Box 228
Prairie Grove, AR 72753

Cataloging-in-Publication Data

Sargent, Dave, 1941-
    Big Jake / by Dave and Pat Sargent ; illustrated by
Jeane Lirley Huff. —Prairie Grove, AR : Ozark
Publishing, ©2003.
    ix, 36 p. : col. ill. ; 21 cm.   (Animal pride series ; 12)
    "I'm very curious"—Cover.
    SUMMARY: Big Jake is a tough little mouse that
has a narrow escape. Includes physical characteristics,
behavior, habitat, and predators of the mouse.
    ISBN: 1-56763-781-7 (hc)
           1-56763-782-5 (pbk)

    1. Mice—Juvenile fiction. [1. Mice—Fiction.] I.
Sargent, Pat, 1936- II. Huff, Jeane Lirley, 1946- ill.
III. Title. IV. Series: Sargent, Dave, 1941- Animal
pride series ; 12.

    PZ10.3.S243Bi 2003
    [Fic]—dc21   96-001501

Factual information excerpted/adapted from
THE WORLD BOOK ENCYCLOPEDIA.
© World Book, Inc. By permission of the publisher.
www.worldbook.com

Printed in the United States of America

iv

Inspired by

the field mice that lived in the fields
on our farm.

Dedicated to

our granddaughter Ashley.

Foreword

Jake is a little mouse who is
very curious. One day he is caught
in the open by a chicken hawk.

Contents

If you would like to have the authors of the Animal Pride Series visit your school, free of charge, call 1-800-321-5671 or 1-800-960-3876.

One

A New Home

Mama Mouse and Daddy Mouse watched the new hay barn going up. They watched with a great interest. They were trying to decide the spot they wanted for their new home.

Mama Mouse and Daddy Mouse usually slept during the warm spring days, but after the terrible storm last week, they had no home. The storm had completely washed away the nest they had shared for the past six months, and now they were looking for a new place.

Mama Mouse watched closely as Farmer John nailed the last board on the back side of the barn. She woke Daddy Mouse and, tugging at his front leg, begged, "Come on, Morse, let's go check out the loft. That's where I want our new home, Morse, in the hayloft."

Morse opened his little black beady eyes and surveyed the almost finished barn. Boy, it sure was high! It would make a real fine home for Matilda and the little ones that would soon be arriving. He would not have to worry anymore.

Matilda scampered toward the barn, then stopped and looked back to see if Morse was coming. When she couldn't see him, she hurried back to find him.

Morse was dozing off again, wishing Matilda would let him be. She twitched her nose and said, "That beats all I have ever in my life seen! It's almost time for my babies to be born and just look at their father! He doesn't seem to care! I'll just have to take care of things myself—as usual!"

She scampered across the field to the new hay barn and, without a moment's hesitation, shot through the door and up the wall to the loft!

Matilda stopped in her tracks, threw her front feet up to her face and said, "Oh, no! There's no hay! I'll never get my nest built in time."

After making her way back to the edge of the woods, she began a frantic search for bird feathers and fur. She knew where to find the fur. She headed straight for a blackberry thicket that was about fifty yards to the south of the new barn.

When Matilda finally reached the berry thicket, she gathered fur from the thorns on the bushes. The thorns had pulled fur from rabbits and other animals that had lived in the thicket or had taken refuge there.

Carrying as much fur as she could hold in her mouth, she made trip after trip to the loft of the new barn. After she placed all the fur in a pile in the corner of the loft, she went searching for small feathers.

She gathered enough feathers to shape her nest and spent the next hour or so lining it with fur. When she finished, she stood back and admired her work.

A sigh escaped Matilda's lips. She knew she had done a fine job. She crawled into the nest and made several turns before curling up for a much-needed nap.

Farmer John's noisy tractor woke Matilda. It sounded like it was coming right into her nest with her. Suddenly a bale of hay landed on the floor of the loft with a thud and a bounce! Matilda squeaked and took off running just as the bale settled next to her nest! She hugged the wall the entire time Farmer John was tossing the bales of hay into the loft.

To her surprise, Farmer John jumped down from the trailer that he had backed into the barn and started up the ladder to the loft and Matilda.

Matilda darted from bale to bale while Farmer John stacked hay

in front of her nest. Then he took a
handkerchief from his pocket and
wiped his brow.

Farmer John climbed down the ladder and up onto his tractor, and Matilda jumped as he started it up. After the sound of the tractor died away, she made her way to her nest. It was completely hidden by the bales of hay, which offered even more security and comfort. Just as she settled in, she felt a sharp twinge and knew it was time—time for her babies to be born.

Just minutes later, after carrying her babies in her tummy for only eighteen days, Matilda looked down and counted, "One, two, three, four, five, six, seven. My word! I have seven new mouths to feed!"

Looking around the big hayloft, she said, "At least I have a nice roomy place to raise them. They'll have lots of room to run and play, and with all the insects, leaves, seeds, and plant stems, they'll have plenty to eat. I feel very fortunate."

While Matilda was admiring her little pink furless babies, Ole Barney the Bear Killer trotted into the new barn to check it out. He sniffed all around, then stopped when he came to the ladder that led to the loft. His nose wiggled; he smelled a mouse!

Barney placed his front feet on the ladder and stretched his neck toward the loft. When he barked softly, Matilda almost jumped out of her skin! She wondered if that ole coonhound could climb ladders! She quietly made her way to the edge of the loft and peeked over.

Below, Barney saw Matilda's long narrow nose with whiskers on it and her beady eyes looking down at him. Then he saw something else. He saw fear in her eyes. At that moment, he caught a special smell that newborn animals give off, and he knew Matilda had new babies. He growled a low warning growl.

Barney knew Farmer John would not want mice living in his new barn. Mice gnawed on wood with their chisel-like teeth, and made holes in walls that other animals could crawl through. If Farmer John stored wheat in the new hay barn, the mice would eat the wheat!

Since Barney couldn't get to the mice, he gave one last growl, as if to say, "You'd better not mess up anything," and trotted out the door.

Two

Chicken Hawk

Matilda scurried back to her nest and counted her babies to make sure they were all there. She knew Barney hadn't bothered them, but his presence made her uneasy. And Barney knew now that she and her babies were living in the hayloft. After hearing others talk about Barney and how he had killed that grizzly, Matilda didn't really feel safe anymore. Not at all.

Ten days later, soft fur covered the tiny baby mice. Matilda already

13

knew which child was going to give her trouble. It was the one who was bigger than all the others—the one she called Big Jake.

Big Jake's legs were just a little longer, his head was a little larger, and his body was a little fatter than the others. This was because he was always nursing. Every time Matilda lay down, Big Jake wanted to eat!

After two weeks had gone by, Matilda woke up one day to see two beady little black eyes staring her right in the face. It startled her so that she jumped straight up in bed. She gasped, "Oh, thank heavens! It's you, Big Jake! I was dreaming about that ole coonhound and just knew he had climbed that ladder."

Big Jake said, "You must be my mama. I can tell by your smell."

Matilda smiled. Now that his eyes were open, she figured Jake would be all over the place. She pointed to her other babies and said, "These are your brothers and sisters, Jake. You are the biggest, so you must help me take care of them."

Big Jake looked at the others. "They can take care of themselves. I'm going hunting. I'm hungry." With food on his mind, he wobbled to the edge of the loft and swayed back and forth, losing his balance.

Big Jake might have fallen, but Matilda was there in a flash. She reached out and grabbed his tail with her sharp teeth and hung on tight.

Big Jake squealed, "Ouch, Mama! That hurts!"

Matilda carried Big Jake over to the nest and put him down. She said, "Don't go near the edge of the loft until you can walk better. If you fall to the ground, it will hurt you."

Matilda had no sooner gotten the words out of her mouth when Jake made another dash for the edge. He gave the ladder a glance, then, teetering and tottering and reeling and rocking, he made his way to the ground below.

Big Jake explored the barn, looking for food. He found nothing that smelled as good as his mama's milk tasted. He was just about to head for the ladder when he noticed a big hole in one of the walls. It was really an open door. As quick as a cat can wink its eye, Big Jake made a dash for the great outdoors.

Matilda had been watching, and when she saw Jake run outside, her front feet flew to her face and she exclaimed, "Mercy me! A hawk will get that boy for sure!" She scampered to the edge of the loft, and half-climbed, half-slid down the wall. When she reached the door, Big Jake was nowhere in sight.

Matilda saw a giant shadow cross the ground. Instinctively, she ran back inside the barn. Just then she heard Big Jake's loud frightened squeak, and she knew that a hawk or an owl, or something was after him.

Matilda knew what she must do. She must sacrifice herself so that her baby might live. The hawk or whatever it was would prefer a big mouse to a little mouse and would eat her instead of Big Jake.

Another squeak and a squawk reached her ears, and she knew that Jake was cornered. His back was against a tree, and his eyes were glowing! Big Jake was mad!

Matilda slid to a halt beside Jake. When he saw his mama, he said, "Get behind me, Mama. I'll protect you!" Then he asked, "What is that thing?"

Searching the sky, Matilda saw the hawk circling for another attack. "It's a hawk! Run!" she screamed. She grabbed him and shoved him under a blackberry thicket.

Big Jake tumbled head over heels! When he stopped, he ran to the edge of the thicket and peeked out. The hawk had given up. It flew over the barn, made a circle, then disappeared behind the trees.

Big Jake sat perfectly still. He wasn't about to move—not until his mama told him it was okay.

Matilda ran to the edge of the thicket and searched the sky and trees with her eyes, knowing the hawk could be on a limb, waiting.

After five minutes had passed, Matilda said, "Jake, when I say go, I want you to run as fast as you can back to the barn! Run up the ladder or up the wall and into our nest. Understand?"

Big Jake asked, "What barn?"

Matilda exclaimed, "Mercy me! I'm talking about that big building over there. That's where our nest is. It's in the hayloft of the red barn. Remember it, because when you come out to play or hunt for food, you must remember where home is."

Big Jake looked the barn over, then said, "Okay, Mama, I'm ready!"

Matilda's eyes swept the sky and the trees, and when she didn't see the hawk, she yelled, "Go!"

Jake scampered across the open space to the hay barn, then Matilda made a dash for the barn. When she reached it, Big Jake was desperately trying to climb the ladder.

Matilda ran up the wall, then hurried over to encourage Jake. They ran to the nest and saw twelve little beady eyes looking at them.

Matilda said, "Look! Your brothers' and sisters' eyes are open."

Big Jake squeaked, "Come on! Let's go play!"

Three

Tractor Ride

Big Jake ran toward the ladder, then stopped and looked back to see if the others were following him. They were nowhere in sight. Being an adventurous little mouse, Jake teetered and tottered and half-slid down the ladder, thinking, "They're no fun. I'll play by myself."

About that time, Big Jake heard the tractor coming. He darted behind a box under Farmer John's workbench that was attached to the west wall of the barn.

Farmer John backed the hay wagon into the barn, then jumped down off the tractor and walked to the back of the wagon. He began picking up the bales and stacking them against the back wall.

Jake peeked out from behind the box, watching Farmer John's every move. Then his eyes focused on the hay wagon. The loose hay on the wagon looked inviting, and Jake was really tired. He waited until Farmer John picked up a bale of hay and turned to place it against the wall, then he scampered to the wagon as fast as his legs could carry him. He ran up the rubber tire, then scratched and clawed his way up onto the wagon bed. Darting around the end of the bales, Jake made his way to the front of the wagon.

Digging down under the loose hay, he curled up into a little tiny round ball and was soon fast asleep.

Big Jake was so tired from all the excitement of being chased by the hawk and his struggle to climb the ladder that he didn't hear the tractor start up. He didn't even feel the gentle sway of the hay wagon when Farmer John drove his tractor, pulling the wagon, home for lunch.

Some time later, Jake opened his eyes. "What was all that jiggling and bouncing?" he wondered. To his amazement, he saw three things jumping up and down on the wagon, throwing loose hay on one another.

Farmer John's daughters were having a big time playing on the hay wagon. They didn't know Big Jake was deep in the hay until he moved. At the sight of the mouse, the girls let out squeals that could be heard all through the woods. Their squeals scared Jake more than the hawk had.

Jake ran to his left, then to his right. No matter which way he ran, there were hands reaching for him.

Big Jake's heart almost stopped beating when something soft and warm closed around him and he felt himself being lifted into the air.

April yelled, "I've got him!" The other girls gathered round to see the little mouse up close.

Over the next few weeks the girls fed Big Jake the milk, cheese, and crumbs Barney left in his dish. They didn't try to pick him up again, so he soon learned to trust them.

Jake liked to climb into April's doll carriage for a nap. One day, when the girls were strolling down the lane that went right past the new hay barn, Big Jake crawled out from under the doll blanket. When he put his front feet on the edge of the doll carriage and looked over, he saw his mama and six young mice huddled at the corner of the big red barn.

A picture of a little mouse and a hawk swooping down from the sky flashed through Big Jake's mind.

Wandering farther from the house than they had ever walked before, the girls had unknowingly brought Big Jake back home.

Big Jake let out a squeak and jumped from the carriage. The girls watched wide-eyed as he ran to the barn where the other mice were.

Matilda nudged Jake several times with her nose, welcoming him home, and then she asked him where in the world he had been.

Jake told his mama and his brothers and sisters all about his adventures. He talked for hours! Finally, Matilda smiled and said to herself, "Big Jake is not only the biggest mouse, but he also has the biggest mouth!"

Four

Mouse Facts

A mouse is a small animal with soft fur, a pointed snout, round black eyes, rounded ears, and a thin tail. Many kinds of rodents (or gnawing animals) are called mice. They include small rats, hamsters, gerbils, harvest mice, grasshopper mice, and deer mice. All these animals have chisel-like front teeth that are useful for gnawing. A rodent's front teeth grow throughout the animal's life.

There are hundreds of kinds of mice, and they live in most parts of the world. They can be found in the mountains, in fields and woodlands, in swamps, near streams, and in deserts. Probably the best known kind of mouse is the house mouse. It lives wherever people live, and often builds its nests in homes, garages, or barns. Some kinds of white house mice are raised as pets. Other kinds are used by scientists to learn about sickness, to test new drugs, and to study behavior.

The word mouse comes from an old Sanskrit word meaning thief. Sanskrit is an ancient language of Asia, where scientists believe house mice originated.

The body of a house mouse is from two and one-half to three and one-half inches long without the tail. The tail is the same length or a little shorter. House mice weigh one-half to one ounce. Their size and weight, and the length of their tails, differ among the varieties and even among individuals of the same variety.

The fur of most house mice is soft, but it may be stiff and wiry. It is grayish brown on the animal's back and sides, and yellowish white underneath.

A mouse can hear well, but it has very poor vision. Mice have strong sharp front teeth that grow throughout the animal's life. With these chisel-like teeth, mice may tear apart packages to get at food inside, gnaw holes in wood, and damage books, clothing, and furniture.

Mice eat such items as glue, leather, paste, and soap. They eat insects and the leaves, roots, seeds, and stems of plants.

A female house mouse may give birth every twenty to thirty days. She carries her young for eighteen to twenty-one days. She has four to seven young at a time. Newborn mice have pink skin and no fur, and their eyes are closed. They are completely helpless.

Soft fur covers their bodies by the time they are ten days old. When they are fourteen days old, their eyes open.

Young mice stay near the nest for about three weeks after birth. Then they leave to build their own nests and start raising families. Most female house mice begin to have young when they are about forty-five days old.

BEYOND "THE END"

LANGUAGE LINKS

Descriptive words make you feel, see, hear, taste, and smell what the author wants you to feel, see, hear, taste, and smell. They create a living picture. Dave and Pat Sargent used many descriptive words to tell about Big Jake's many adventures. Make a list of all the descriptive words in the story such as, "teetering, tottering, reeling, and rocking" as Big Jake made his way down the ladder. Can't you see that funny picture in your mind? Find many others.

CURRICULUM CONNECTIONS

If Mama Mouse was 45 days old when she had her first 7 baby mice and can have 7 more every 20 days, how many babies will she have if she lives 1 year?

Divide class into 3 groups with 9 students in each group. Give each group a bowl of dry beans. Lead the children to know there are 365 days in a year. They must first take away the 45 days it took for Mama Mouse to have her first 7 babies—leaving a balance of 320 days. One student in each group counts out 7 beans and puts them in a pile. How many 20-day blocks are in 320 days? (16) Have the other 8 students in each group count out 2 piles of beans with 7 in each pile. Now there should be

17 piles of beans. Count the beans in all 17 piles. MAMA MOUSE COULD HAVE 119 BABIES IN ONE YEAR!

Scientists use mice in their labs to learn about sickness, to test new drugs, and to study behavior. Dr. Mary MacDougall of the University of Texas Health Science Center in San Antonio is involved in research to make custom-made human teeth. The first step of the research is to study how mouse teeth grow and develop in the laboratory. To read about this interesting study, go to web site <www.askjeeves.com>. Type in the question: WHAT ABOUT MOUSE TEETH? Select the #1 result, "BBC News/SCI/Tech/ Mouse teeth grown in lab".

THE ARTS

With a soft music background, have students stand and as teacher calls out descriptive words found in the story of Big Jake, ask them to pantomime the movements the words "paint" in their minds.

THE BEST I CAN BE

You are not likely to be eaten by a hawk when you choose not to follow your mother's instructions, but there are consequences. Discuss the consequences of not listening to your mother's (or your teacher's) directions.